DATE DUE			
JUL 06 1993	MAR 1 3		JUN 2 4 2008
OCT 06	MAY 2 5 1995		
DEC 9	APR 0 5 1996		
FEB 08	JUL 3 0 1996		
	JAN 1 9 1999		
MAR 1 0 1994	FEB 0 2 1999		
MAY 0 4 1994	OCT 2 2 2000		
JAN 1 2 1995	JUN 2 2000 2002		
	JAN 1 9 2002		
JUL 1 2 1995	JUN 2 7 2003		

MY MOM CAN'T READ

MURIEL STANEK

pictures by JACQUELINE ROGERS

ALBERT WHITMAN & COMPANY, NILES, ILLINOIS

To Aileen P. Moore, a great teacher. **M.S.**

Library of Congress Cataloging in Publication Data

Stanek, Muriel.
  My mom can't read.

  Summary: When Tina asks her mother for help in
first-grade reading, she discovers to her shock that
her mother can't read. A concerned teacher helps them
to find tutors and they both learn to read together.
  [1. Reading – Fiction.   2. Illiteracy – Fiction.
3. Mothers and daughters – Fiction] I. Rogers,
Jackie, ill. II. Title.
  PZ7.S78637Mz 1986   [Fic]   86-1637
  ISBN 0-8075-5343-3 (lib. bdg.)

The text of this book is set in fourteen-point Garth Graphic.

Text © 1986 by Muriel Stanek
Illustrations © 1986 by Jacqueline Rogers
Published in 1986 by Albert Whitman & Company, Niles, Illinois
Published simultaneously in Canada by General Publishing, Limited, Toronto

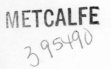

The day I started first grade,
my teacher, Mrs. Hall,
gave everyone a brand-new orange reader.
I could hardly wait to show my book to Mom.

When I got home, I asked,
"Will you help me read, Mom?"
She nodded. "After supper."

While Mom set the table,
I looked at my book.
Carefully, I turned each page so that I wouldn't tear it.
When I had looked all through the book,
I started over again.

After supper we sat together holding my book.
"Read it, read it!" I said to Mom.

Slowly she began telling me about the pictures,
the way she always did.
"What do the words say?" I asked.
"Tell me the words."

"Not tonight," she answered.
"It's time for bed now, Tina."

The next day, Mrs. Hall gave us letters in long envelopes.
"Please give these letters to your parents," she said.
"They are about your health records.
Bring the answer back tomorrow."

I told Mom the letter was important.
"I'll take care of it," she said.
But she put the envelope on the kitchen shelf
without opening it.

Each day I had to go to school without the answer
because Mom was too busy to write one.
And each day my teacher asked for it.
I felt awful!

Then, one morning, I cried,
"I can't go to school without an answer!"
Mom took the envelope,
and we walked to school very early,
before she went to work.

"Can you help me with this paper?" Mom asked Mrs. Hall.
"I broke my glasses and can't see the words."

I almost said, "You don't have glasses, Mom."
But she gave me a look that meant "be quiet."
So I sat on the floor and looked at books.

Mom answered the questions my teacher read to her.
Then Mrs. Hall said, "Tina needs her booster shots.
The Public Health Center downtown gives free shots."
Mom said she would take me there.

Early Saturday morning we started out for the Health Center.
"I wonder if this bus goes downtown," Mom said.
But when she asked the driver, he yelled,
"Read the sign, lady!
This bus goes to the airport.
Take the one over there."

We got on the right bus, and this time the driver was nice.
He said he'd point out the Health Center for us.

It was a big building with many doors and elevators.
A sign on the wall had lots of words and numbers.
Mom looked at the sign for a while.
"Does it tell where to go?" I asked.
"It's hard to read," she answered.

We asked people where you got booster shots,
but nobody knew.
Finally a nurse showed us.
After we waited a long, long time,
the doctor gave me my shots.
And I hardly cried at all.

Mom said I deserved a treat.
"Do we have enough money?" I asked. "Yes," she replied.
So we stopped for lunch in a little restaurant next door.
"Let's read the menu," I said to Mom.
"Oh, let's just have hamburgers," she said
as she closed the menu.

After lunch, we saw a bus at the corner.
"What does the sign say?" I asked Mom,
but she didn't hear me.
Instead, she asked the driver,
"Does this bus go to Lowe Avenue?"
When the driver said, "Yes, ma'am,"
we hurried on to get a seat by the window.

The bus rode a long, long way,
past places we hadn't seen when we came downtown.

"This isn't the right way," Mom said finally.
"We've gone too far."

She went up to the driver.
"Are you sure you're going to South Lowe Avenue?" she asked.
"No," he answered. "I'm going to North Lowe Avenue.
You didn't say you wanted to go south.
You'll have to get off and ride the other way."

A storm was coming, and the sky was dark.
It began to rain as we hurried to the corner
where the driver pointed.
The stop was near a small park, almost empty now.

We stood alone in the rain.
There were no buildings for shelter.

I was tired, and my arm started to hurt.
"We should have read the sign before we got on that bus,"
I told Mom. "Then we wouldn't be lost way out here."

"I know, I know," she said.
"I'm sorry this turned out to be such a terrible day.
We'll have hot chocolate when we get home."

As soon as we got on the bus, I put my head
on Mom's shoulder and closed my eyes.
When I woke up, it was time to get off.

The rain had stopped.
We were home, at last.
It had been a long, hard day for both of us.
But I had the paper from the doctor
to bring to school on Monday.

I liked Mrs. Hall, and I liked school.
But each day reading was getting harder and harder.
Most of the kids were starting the blue book.
I was still in the orange book—the easy one.

"Maybe your mother can help you," Mrs. Hall said.
"Here are worksheets and another book
for you to study at home."

When I told Mom I was having trouble with reading,
she looked upset.
"You must work harder, Tina," she told me.
I began to cry.
"But I'm working as hard as I can.
Please help me," I begged.

Mom put her arms around me.
There were tears in her eyes.
"Oh, Tina, I want to help you,
but I can't read! I only pretend."

"You can't read?" I said.
"I thought all grown-ups could read."
"No," Mom told me,
"your grandma and grandpa can't read, either.
We moved around a lot, and I missed school."

"Can't you learn?" I asked.
"I don't know," Mom said.
"I've never tried since I've been grown-up.
I'm too ashamed to ask for help."

That night I couldn't sleep.
Now I knew why Mom pretended to have broken glasses,
why we don't have books at home like other people,
and why she couldn't read signs when we went downtown.

When my teacher asked if
Mom was helping me with reading,
I shook my head.
"Is there a problem?" she asked.
I didn't want to tell her at first.
But then I whispered in her ear,
"My mom can't read."

"Don't worry, Tina," she said softly.
"We'll find a way to help you."

Mrs. Hall called Mom to tell her about reading classes
after school and on Saturdays at the Community Center.
"Perhaps you could take Tina there for help," she suggested.

"Yes, I'll take her tomorrow," Mom said.
"Do they help grown-ups learn to read there, too?"
Mom crossed her fingers and winked at me.
"I have a friend who wants to learn to read."

"Yes," answered my teacher,
"they have wonderful classes for adults.
Take your friend along when you bring Tina."

The next day after school we walked to the Community Center.
I went into a reading class with five other children.
James and Meagan from my class were there, too.

Mom got a tutor for reading.
A tutor is someone who helps one person at a time.

On our way home, Mom said,
"When I can read, maybe I'll be able to get a better job."
"And we'll each get a library card and take out books," I told her.
"We'll be able to read directions on signs and boxes
and medicine bottles, too," Mom said.
"And I'll never have to pretend to read again."

Now every night Mom and I do our homework together.
We get the newspaper and pick out
the words and sentences we know.
Sometimes it's hard, but we're getting better.

We make all kinds of signs and read them to each other.
"One day we'll go downtown without getting lost," I told Mom.
"And we'll order lunch from the menu," she said, smiling.

Today I left a note on Mom's dresser.
She was happy when she saw it.
It was the first note I ever wrote,
and the first Mom ever read.

METCALFE